❤ HANS MY HEDGEHOG ❤

HANS MY HEDGEHOG

A TALE FROM
the
brothers
Grimm

RETOLD BY

KATE COOMBS

ILLUSTRATED BY

JOHN NICKLE

atheneum books for young readers
NEW YORK LONDON TORONTO SYDNEY

ATHENEUM BOOKS FOR YOUNG READERS
An imprint of Simon & Schuster Children's Publishing Division
1230 Avenue of the Americas, New York, New York 10020
Text copyright © 2012 by Kate Coombs
Illustrations copyright © 2012 by John Nickle
For information about special discounts for bulk purchases, please
contact Simon & Schuster Special Sales at 1-866-506-1949 or
business@simonandschuster.com.
The Simon & Schuster Speakers Bureau can bring authors to your live
event. For more information or to book an event, contact the Simon
& Schuster Speakers Bureau at 1-866-248-3049 or visit our website at
www.simonspeakers.com.
Book design by Debra Sfetsios-Conover
The text for this book is set in Abelard.
The illustrations for this book are rendered in acrylic.
Manufactured in China
1111 SCP
First Edition
10 9 8 7 6 5 4 3 2 1
Library of Congress Cataloging-in-Publication Data
Coombs, Kate.
Hans My Hedgehog / Kate Coombs ; illustrated by John Nickle. —
1st ed.
p. cm.
Summary: Riding a rooster and playing magical music on his fiddle, a
young man, who is half hedgehog, half human, wins the hand of a
beautiful princess.
ISBN 978-1-4169-1533-1
ISBN 978-1-4424-4720-2 (eBook)
 [1. Fairy tales. 2. Folklore—Germany.] I. Nickle, John, ill. II. Grimm,
Jacob, 1785–1863. III. Grimm, Wilhelm, 1786–1859. IV. Hans mein Igel.
English. V. Title.
PZ8.C7882Han 2011
398.2—dc22
[E]
2006019311

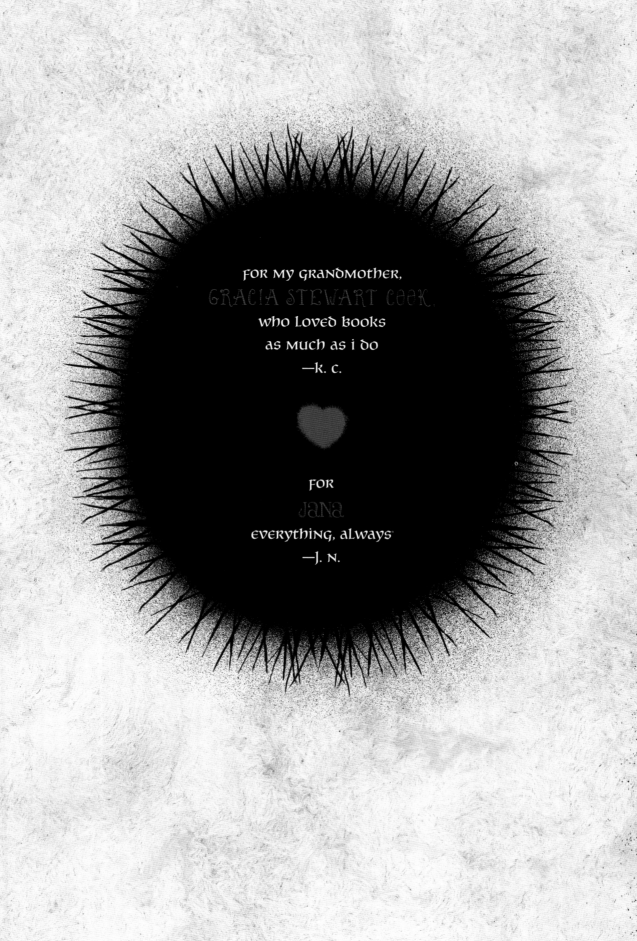

FOR MY GRANDMOTHER,
GRACIA STEWART COOK,
who loved books
as much as i do
—k. c.

FOR
JANA
everything, always
—J. N.

Once upon a time in a village just past yonder, there lived a prosperous farmer and his wife.

Their fields were full of wheat, their chickens laid egg after egg like so many silver coins, and their pigs were fat and contented.

But they had no children to bless their home.

The couple so longed for a child
that one day the man cried,
"I want a son even if he's half a hedgehog!"

The next spring the farmer's wife gave birth
to a child who was exactly that—
a boy from the waist down
and a hedgehog from the waist up.

"You've cursed our little one!"
the farmwife scolded.
But she was a mother just the same,
so she wrapped her prickly baby in a thick quilt
and called him Hans My Hedgehog.

As Hans grew older, he began to help around the farm. He was especially good with the pigs. They followed him even when Hans stole off to the great and magical forest. Other folk lost their way there, but not Hans.

One morning Hans heard distant music shivering through the trees. He went straight home and told his father how he longed to make music of his own.

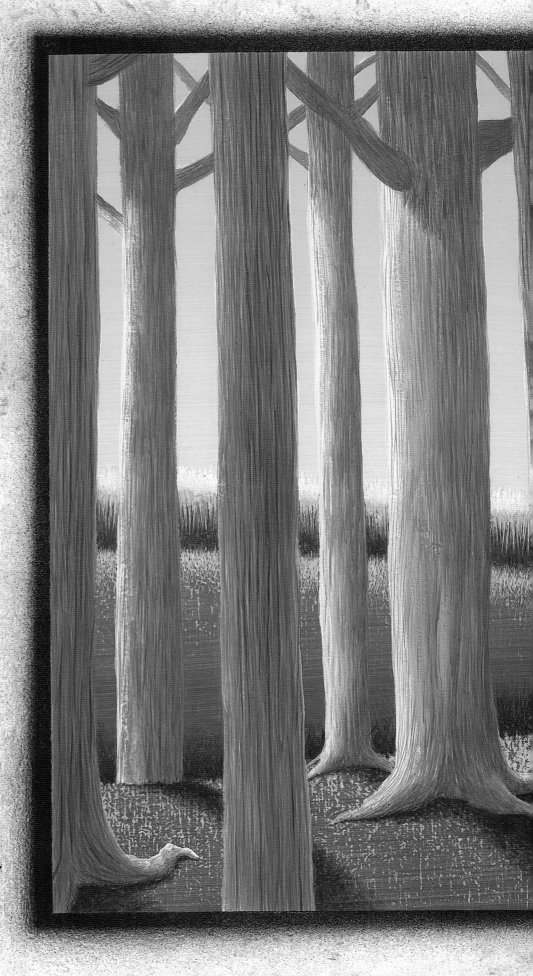

The next time the farmer traveled
to the market fair, he brought home
a finely made fiddle for his son.

Hans practiced and practiced,
and the pigs gathered 'round him to listen.

In time he was asked to play for
the village dances. But when he put down
his bow, the village girls went off
with the village boys, leaving the
fiddler alone.

Hans became quiet and sad.
At last he went to his father and said,
"Saddle the biggest rooster in the barnyard,
for I'm flying to the forest to live
with my pigs."

Nothing his mother or father could say
would change his mind. Away went Hans,
with his fiddle under his arm and every
one of his pigs running along behind him.

"Good-bye, Hans My Hedgehog!"
called his mother.

Deep and deeper into the enchanted
wood Hans traveled, until he found
a spot to make his home.

Then every day he would fly on
his rooster to the top of a tall tree
to practice the fiddle.

Each note slipped between
the trees like a spell.
The pigs, listening below,
were steeped in magic.

One morning a king and his retinue
lost their way in the forest.
At last they heard the eerie sound
of Hans's fiddle. They followed
the tune to a tall tree, where
they saw a strange creature high
above their heads.

"You there!" called the king.
"Can you show us our way?"

"I will," Hans said, "if you agree
to give me the first thing that meets you
when you reach your palace."

"Anything," said the king,
so Hans left his tree and
his pigs to lead the royal
party out of the wood.
For hours they walked.
At last Hans brought the
grumbling monarch and
his men to the wide road
at the edge of the forest.

When the king reached his palace and the
gates swung open, the first thing he saw
was his only daughter running to meet him

He frowned, telling her the tale of the youth who was half a hedgehog. "Of course, I would never give you to such a creature," he said.

"Well, I would never go!" snapped the princess.

So the king commanded his gatekeeper that if a man who was half a hedgehog should appear, he was to be turned away without fail.

But Hans had already forgotten the king's promise, so busy was he with his fiddle and his pigs. *Come here, sleep, twirl, play hide-and-seek*: Hans's clever pigs learned to obey each tune he played.

Some months later another king and his attendants lost their way in the forest. They, too, followed the notes of the fiddle to Hans and asked for his help.

"I'll show you the way," said Hans, "if you agree to give me the first thing that meets you when you reach your palace."

"You have my word," said the second king.

Then Hans led the king and his men from the heart of the wild wood to the safety of the road.

When the king came to his palace gates, his own lovely daughter ran to meet him. With a sigh, he told her what had happened. "How can I give you to such a creature?" he asked.

"You are a man of your word," said the princess. "I will honor your promise."

So the second king instructed his gatekeeper that if a man who was half a hedgehog should appear, he was to be welcomed graciously into the palace.

Not long afterward, Hans heard a third cry
for help from his lofty perch. He came
down again and found a ragged old woman.

Hans took her bags on his back,
showing her the way out of the forest.
This time he did not ask anything in return.

"You're a good lad," said the old woman,
"so I will give you some news.
It is said that two kings lost their way
in these very woods and were rescued
in exchange for a promise.
When they came safely home,
they were met by their own daughters,
two princesses."

"That is news indeed," said Hans My
Hedgehog.

Then he hurried back to his tall tree to saddle his rooster. Hans played a lively tune, and his pigs came running. Arranging themselves into piggy ranks like a small army, they marched after Hans out of the forest and on to the first king's palace.

The gatekeeper tried to turn Hans away, but Hans on his rooster flew right over the gate, and his pigs poured past the gatekeeper into the courtyard.

"King!" Hans called. "I have come for
your daughter!"

The king stuck his head out a window.
"Certainly not!" he told Hans.

The princess poked her head out
another window.
"I won't do it!" she shrieked.

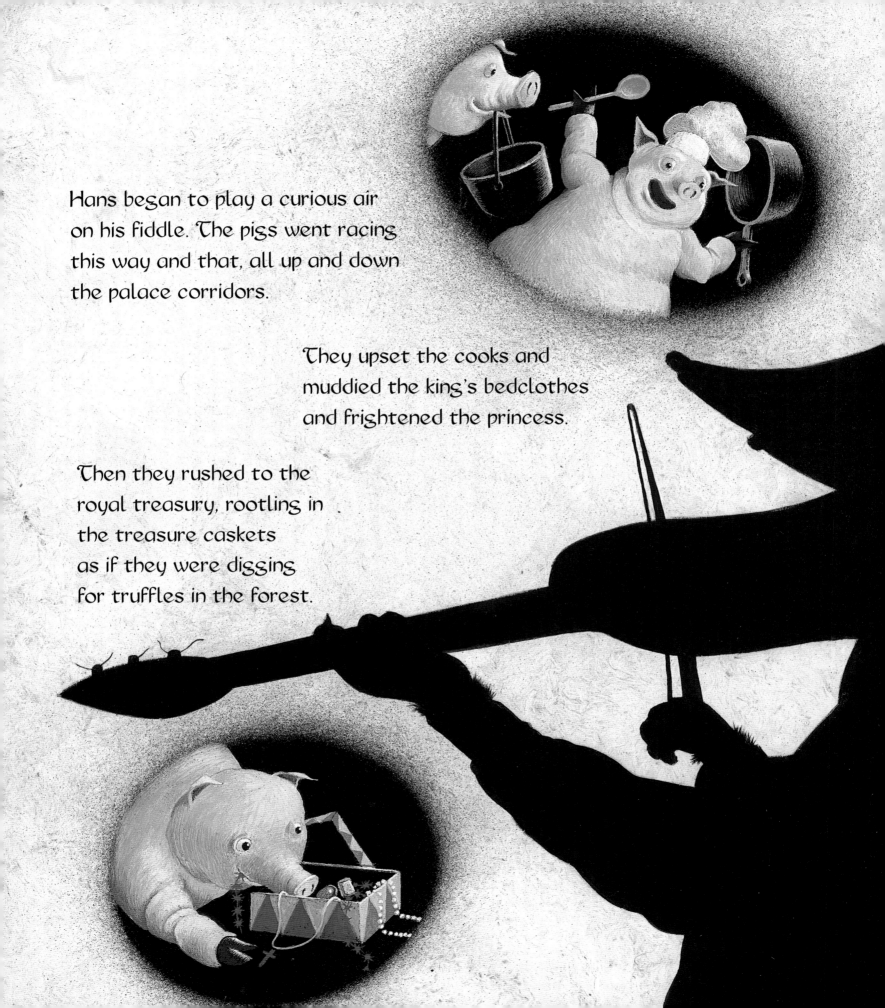

Hans began to play a curious air
on his fiddle. The pigs went racing
this way and that, all up and down
the palace corridors.

They upset the cooks and
muddied the king's bedclothes
and frightened the princess.

Then they rushed to the
royal treasury, rootling in
the treasure caskets
as if they were digging
for truffles in the forest.

"Call off your pigs!" the king howled. "You can have my daughter!"

But Hans shook his head. "I don't want her."

And when he and his pigs left
the palace, they took half the
king's fortune with them.

"Off we go!" said Hans, and
so they journeyed to the palace
of the second king.

This time the gatekeeper let
Hans right in. "King!" Hans
announced. "I have come for
your daughter!"

The second king bowed.
"A promise is a promise,"
he said.

The princess stepped forward.
"And I have agreed,"
she told Hans.

The king sent his own
carriage for Hans's
mother and father.
How they gasped
and gaped to see their
son in such a place!

The palace
seamstress made
them clothes for
the wedding, and of
course she sewed a
velvet suit for Hans,
though he struggled
to fit it over
his quills.

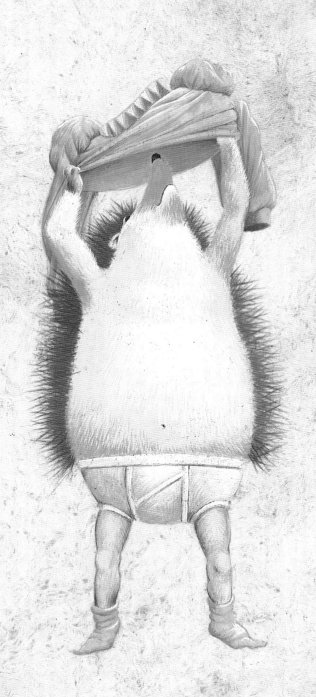

The day of the wedding, guests came from near and far. Tables were piled high with tarts and trifles and turnovers, and little fruit trees were rolled in on carts.

A dozen musicians played for the dance—but when Hans began to play his fiddle, the other musicians put down their instruments to listen.

First Hans played so joyfully that elderly
courtiers stopped nodding off and began to
jig and prance with the best of them.

Then Hans played so sweetly that
everyone in the palace grew teary.
Birds came calling in through
the windows, their music joining
the song of the fiddle.

Finally Hans played so
magically that the palace walls
trembled. He played so
magically that his hedgehog
skin tugged and crumpled
around him. With that, Hans
fell to the floor and
the music stopped.

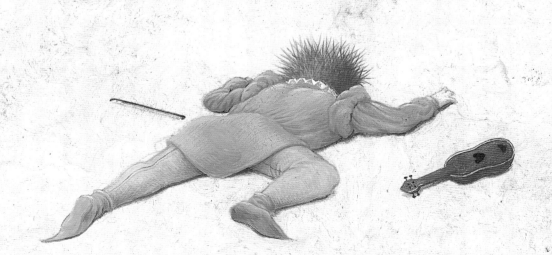

"Why, Hans My Hedgehog!"
the princess cried, helping him up.

But he was a hedgehog no more,
not even half a hedgehog,
for the long-ago curse was broken.

Hans stood before them all,
a goodly young man with a rare
and wonderful smile for
his new bride.

As for who wept more tears
of happiness, the farmer or his wife,
it's hard to say!

AUTHOR'S NOTE

Hans-My-Hedgehog is one of the fairy tales collected by the
Brothers Grimm, and you will find that I've taken some liberties with my
retelling. In the original, Hans's parents are unloving, Hans brings his pig
herd back to the village to be slaughtered, and Hans treats the first
princess very badly. His spell is broken when the second princess steals
his hedgehog skin while he is sleeping and throws it in the fire, but
this makes him very ill for a long time.

Instead, I have chosen to give Hans kind parents and make the pigs
the instrument of his revenge against the first king. I was also intrigued
by Hans's musical ability, although he plays the bagpipes in
the Grimms's version. When illustrator John Nickle suggested
changing the bagpipes to a fiddle, I was happy to agree because a fiddler
is often a magical character in folktales.

Hans's loneliness and courage touched me a great deal. He is clearly
a misfit, but he takes charge of his destiny and makes the best life he
can even before the kings show up. As you can see, I liked the thought
that Hans could turn his misfortune into magic through the power of his
music, as well as through his ordinary longing to be loved.